RUGBY BLOXAM COUNTY MIDDLE SCHOOL

Text copyright © 1991 Catherine Robinson

First published in Great Britain in 1991
by Simon & Schuster Young Books
Reprinted in 1991 and 1993

Photoset in 14/23 Souvenir Light by
Goodfellow & Egan, Cambridge

Colour origination by
Scantrans Pte Ltd, Singapore

Printed and bound in Belgium by
Proost International Book Productions

Simon & Schuster Young Books
Campus 400
Maylands Avenue
Hemel Hempstead HP2 7EZ

BRITISH LIBRARY CATALOGUING IN PUBLICATION DATA
Robinson, Catherine
Mog and Bumble.
1. English Language. *Readers*
I. Title   II. Englander, Alice
428.6

ISBN 0-7500-0579-3
ISBN 0-7500-0580-7 Pbk

Catherine Robinson

MOG and BUMBLE

Illustrated by Alice Englander

SIMON & SCHUSTER
YOUNG BOOKS

For Alexander

1

Mog came to live with the Smiths a long time ago. They found him fast asleep among the packing cases and boxes when they first moved in to their house. It was snowing, and they hadn't the heart to put him out again. Then Mum gave him a saucer of milk, and that was that; he was there for good. If he'd once had another home, he never went back to it, and nobody ever came looking for him.

All this had happened such a long time ago that Sarah couldn't remember a time when Mog wasn't living with them.

"I can," said William. "I remember before he came."

Sarah scoffed. "You can't! You weren't even born then."

Sarah was Mog's little girl. They were special friends. Mog would even let Sarah tickle his tummy, which Mum said a lot of cats wouldn't put up with. And in return, Sarah would tell him what a wonderful, beautiful, extra-special cat he was.

He wasn't really.
He was just an ordinary
tabby cat with a
white bib and paws.
He was a bit battered
about the ears, because
he didn't like other cats
very much and was
always getting into
fights. And over the
last winter or two the
Smiths had noticed
him limping.

"He's got rheumatism," Dad told them. "He's getting old." But he was still beautiful to Sarah.

One day, Mum and Dad and Sarah and William all went for a ride in the car. Mum and Dad wouldn't tell Sarah and William where they were going. They just smiled at each other from time to time.

At last, the car drew up outside a big house. Sarah could hear masses and masses of dogs, all barking at once.

"Why have we come here?" she asked Mum. "What is this place, anyway?"

"It's the RSPCA," Mum told her, still smiling. "They look after lost dogs and cats, and find homes for them."

William started to jump around with excitement. "Yah-hoo!" he shouted. He knew why they'd come. "We're getting a dog! We're getting a dog!" And Sarah could see from Mum and Dad's faces that it was true.

William had been asking for a dog for ages, but
Mum and Dad had never said anything except "We'll
see." Sarah hated it when they said that. She knew it
usually meant "No." But this time, it must have
meant "Yes." At first, Sarah didn't like the idea very
much. She wasn't sure how Mog would feel about
having a dog around the place. But when she saw
the dogs, she changed her mind.

As the Smiths walked up and down the concrete paths, trying to choose one, all the dogs came right up to the wire netting. They wagged their tails and pressed their wet noses through the holes in the fence. Some of them even jumped up and down, eager to be chosen as William's dog. Sarah would have liked to have taken them all home, but she knew they couldn't. She didn't like to think about what might happen to the dogs they didn't choose.

William finally picked one. It was a puppy, with soft-looking fluffy brown fur. One ear stood up straight while the other sort of flopped over one eye. The other eye had a white patch around it.

"Isn't he cute?" William yelled with pleasure.

Dad agreed he was. "Look at him bumbling along; he knows he's going home with you!"

Mum and Dad sorted things out with the RSPCA man. Then they drove home, with the new puppy on William's lap in the back of the car.

"You'll have to think of a name for him," Mum told William. "How about Patch? That's a good name."

William shook his head. "No. His name's Bumble."

Mog was waiting at the front door when the Smiths got home. He stood up and stretched when he saw them. He rubbed his head around Sarah's legs and miaowed to be let in. He didn't see William carrying Bumble.

Mum opened the front door, and William put
Bumble down on the ground. The puppy ran
straight past Mog and into the kitchen, where he
found Mog's food on the floor. He bounced over to
it and swallowed it all down with a glooping sound.
Then he stuck his nose in Mog's milk, and glooped
that down too.

Mog stared at the puppy in amazement. But the
amazement didn't last for long. He arched his back
and fluffed up his fur and puffed up his tail like a
brush, and hissed fiercely at Bumble. Bumble had
never seen a cross cat before, and thought Mog was
playing. He bumbled round him, wagging his little
tail with pleasure. Mog hissed again, and when
Bumble got too close he lifted a paw and whacked
the puppy around the ear.

Bumble yelped with fright as he rolled over and over, head over tail. He ended up in a crumpled little heap by the back door.

"Bumble!" William yelled, upset. "Naughty cat, Mog!" And he went to smack him.

But Mum stopped him. "Don't do that, William," she said. "They're going to have to get used to each other. Mog's bound to be annoyed at first."

Sarah picked Mog up to soothe him, and William picked up Bumble. But neither of them would be soothed. Mog was still fluffed up and cross. He scratched Sarah for the very first time as he wriggled and wroggled and tried to escape from her arms. And Bumble was so scared by his close encounter with this strange spitting thing that he made a puddle, all down William's shirt.

"Oh Bumble," William said sadly, as Mum led him away to be changed.

"Oh Mog," Sarah whispered, as she sucked her scratched hand. She knew it had been an accident, but it still hurt. But the hurt was more inside her than on her hand. She wondered if Mog and Bumble would ever get used to each other, as Mum had said. It hadn't been a very good start.

4

It didn't carry on very well, either. For weeks, whenever the puppy appeared, bumbling innocently along, Mog would hiss and cuff Bumble around the ear. So Mum gave them beds in separate rooms; Bumble in the kitchen, and Mog in luxury on the spare room bed.

"That cat is spoilt," Dad grumbled.

"He's upset," Sarah said firmly, burying her face in Mog's purring silky side. "He has to get used to Bumble."

"Bumble has to get used to Mog, too," William said. "He keeps bashing him. Why does he keep bashing him, Mummy?"

But Mum had no real answer.

Mog soon grew tired of bashing Bumble. He
started hiding behind doors instead and then leaping
out at the puppy, doubled in size and hissing and
spitting like a whole Bonfire Night of fireworks.
Bumble soon stopped trotting happily along. He
began to look nervously about him as he went. The
whole family was getting fed up with Mog disturbing
the household.

"That cat's a menace," Dad grumbled. Privately, Sarah was beginning to agree with him. But she would never tell that to Mog.

Bumble was a bit of a menace, too. He kept digging up the plants in the garden and eating them. And he didn't understand that he was supposed to go outside to do his puddles and things. Mum was getting very fed up with cleaning them up off the carpet.

"They're *both* menaces," she grumbled one day. She was on her hands and knees yet again with a bucket of hot water, strong with disinfectant. "I can't stand much more of this. One of them will have to go."

Nobody thought she really meant it, not even Mum. She was just cross at forever having to clean up Bumble's messes and cope with Mog's fireworks. But later on, Sarah remembered Mum's words, and wondered if Mog had overheard.

5

It was a lovely bright sunny Sunday, and Dad decided they would all take Bumble for a walk.

"We'll go to the park," he declared. "Get some fresh air. And we can teach Bumble to fetch sticks."

Mum laughed, and called Dad an optimist. Sarah didn't know what that meant, but they both sounded happy. It was the first time Mum had laughed like that since Bumble had come to live with them.

So off they went. Dad had Bumble on his new
lead. Sarah was wearing her Christmas present scarf
and gloves, and William had on his new shiny red
wellington boots, which he kept stopping to admire.

Suddenly, Sarah realised that Mog was following
them. He'd never done that before; he didn't usually
want to be anywhere near Bumble.

"Go home, Mog!" she told him. And then, more crossly, "Go home! You can't come to the park with us – go home!"

But still Mog followed them, trailing behind and hiding in bushes, and then running fast to catch them up. Sarah was worried because they had to cross a main road to get to the park. Cars and buses and lorries whizzed along it, and she knew that Mog didn't realise you were supposed to use the zebra crossing to get to the other side. She didn't even think Mog knew what zebra crossings were. She had once seen him sit down in the middle of their road to

have a little wash, and not move out of the way even when a car came. The driver had to get out of the car and pick Mog up. He set him down on the side of the road, and Mog had continued with his wash, quite unbothered.

"Make him go home, Mum," Sarah said, concerned.

But Mum told her to ignore him. "He'll soon go home by himself," she said. And she seemed to be right. Mog stayed on the right side of the busy main road, and when they finished their walk in the park and came back, there was no sign of him.

6

That afternoon, Sarah went to play at her friend Sophie's house. When she got back home, she felt that something wasn't quite right. But it wasn't until supper time that she realised what it was.

"Where's Mog?" she asked Mum. "Have you seen him?"

"Why, no," Mum replied. "Now you come to mention it. Let me put his supper down; that'll soon make him appear."

But it didn't. And he hadn't appeared by the time
William went to bed, or at Sarah's bedtime either.

When William was very little he had once lost
Albert, his teddy. He had cried for three days until
Albert turned up at the back of the airing cupboard,
where he had pushed him and then forgotten about
him.

Now Sarah knew how he had felt. She wandered around the house with a lump in her throat, calling Mog, although she knew he wasn't there and couldn't hear her. She even made Mum look in the airing cupboard, remembering Albert. But Mog wasn't there.

Dad went into the garden with a torch, and looked
in the shed and the garage, but Mog wasn't there
either. Then Dad put his coat on and walked up to
the main road by the park. Sarah knew where he
had gone, although nobody told her. She imagined
Mog's furry tabby body squashed in a sad heap on
the road.

But when Dad came back he didn't have Mog with
him, squashed or otherwise. He shook his head.

"I'm sorry, Sarah," he said softly. "There's no sign of him."

Mum bustled around her and took her up to bed. She made her some cocoa. She even read her a story and tucked her in with a kiss, like she used to, when Sarah was younger.

"Cheer up, sweetheart," she said gently, stroking the hair from Sarah's forehead. "Mog will be all right. He's a wise old cat. He can look after himself, just you wait and see."

34

But Sarah didn't believe her. She lay in bed once Mum had turned the light off, with tears rolling down her face and a nasty tight feeling in her throat. All she could hear were Mum's words; "One of them will have to go."

7

Sarah woke up very early the next morning. It was so early it was still dark. For a moment she just lay there, half asleep. Then she remembered; Mog.

She fell out of bed and stumbled down the stairs, and opened the front door. The street lamp lit up the road with a ghostly orange glow. There was nobody about; no cars, no people. No Mog.

"Mog!" she called, in a whisper. "Oh, Mog! Where are you?"

But he didn't come running to her.

Sarah shivered on the doorstep. She closed the door and went back upstairs, although she didn't want to. She got back into bed and lay awake for ages, thrashing around and thinking terrible thoughts about poor lost Mog. At last she fell asleep.

She was woken again when it was properly morning, by the sound of Mum going downstairs. Sarah ran down the stairs after her.

"Mum," she called, but quietly. She didn't want to wake Dad and William. "Do you think . . ."

Then she stopped. Mum had opened the door to bring the milk in; and there, on the doorstep next to the three pints, sat Mog! He ran in, miaowing.

Sarah gasped with happiness. She couldn't speak. She just picked him up and cuddled him and kissed him. Mum kissed Sarah, and smiled at them both.

"You see," she said, later on. "I knew he'd come back!"

"So did I," said Sarah. "So did I, really."

"Where do you think he's been?" William wanted to know at breakfast. "What's he been doing? Where did he sleep?"

"He's had a night on the tiles, that's all," Dad said. "No harm done. He knows home's the best place to be."

Sarah thought a night on the tiles sounded uncomfortable. She got Mum to open a tin of tuna as a special breakfast for Mog.

"That cat's a glutton," said Dad. But he looked pleased Mog was back, all the same.

Everyone was pleased to see Mog; even Bumble,
who wagged his tail happily when Sarah put Mog
down. Sarah and William thought they might be
friends now. But Mog puffed up in his usual way,
and would have bashed Bumble if Sarah hadn't
hastily picked him up to give him another 'welcome
home' cuddle. She had thought he'd run away
because he hated Bumble, and didn't want to live
with the Smiths any more. But now he was back. To
Sarah, that was all that mattered.

8

Later that afternoon, Bumble was out in the garden. He had his lead on, and it was attached to the washing line. Dad had discovered that he could still run around like that, but he couldn't get at the plants and eat them.

All of a sudden, there was a tremendous woofing from the garden; "I thought it was a billion dogs," Sarah said afterwards.

"I thought it was a trillion," said William, not to be outdone.

In actual fact, it was only two dogs; but they were very big. They had jumped over the fence at the bottom of the garden and were barking fiercely at poor Bumble, who was still tied to the washing line. He was a little shivering heap on the ground.

"Mummy!" yelled William, bursting into tears.

"Dad!" shrieked Sarah. "Come quickly! They're killing Bumble!"

But before Mum or Dad could do anything, a flash of tabby lightning came bursting from the rose bushes. It was Mog. He whirled around, hissing and spitting and flashing his claws.

The dogs had never seen anything like it. They were used to chasing cats, not the other way around. They fled in fright, leaping over the fence much quicker than they had leapt in.

Mum, Dad, William and Sarah all went into the garden. Dad untied Bumble, who jumped up and tried to lick everybody's face. Now the big dogs had gone, he was ready to play again.

Mog was sitting on the ground, back to his normal size. He washed his ears carefully, and ignored the puppy.

"Mog saved Bumble!" William beamed. "Isn't he brilliant!"

"Fancy standing up to those dogs like that!" Dad exclaimed. "That cat's a marvel!"

"He certainly is," agreed Mum. "Perhaps he's at last accepted Bumble's here to stay."

Sarah didn't say anything. She just picked Mog up, and buried her face in his fur. She was very proud of him.

PRINTED IN BELGIUM BY

proost
INTERNATIONAL BOOK PRODUCTION